NOV 20

W9-AYS-950

*For Leovander, who is nearly always
full of the joys of spring!*
~ S. S.

*For Kathryn, my dancing, surfing, and
singing partner in crime, and fellow foodie!*
~ C. P.

IOWA CITY
PUBLIC LIBRARY

IOWA CITY
PUBLIC
LIBRARY
Friends
FOUNDATION

**THIS IS ONE OF THE
3,500 PICTURE BOOKS**

MADE POSSIBLE BY GENEROUS FINANCIAL GIFTS TO
THE IOWA CITY PUBLIC LIBRARY
FRIENDS FOUNDATION

Tiger Tales
5 River Road, Suite 128, Wilton, CT 06897
Published in the United States 2020
Originally published in Great Britain 2020
by Little Tiger Press Ltd.
Text copyright © 2020 Steve Smallman
Illustrations copyright © 2020 Caroline Pedler
ISBN-13: 978-1-68010-188-1
ISBN-10: 1-68010-188-9
Printed in China
LTP/1400/2933/0919
All rights reserved
10 9 8 7 6 5 4 3 2 1

For more insight and activities, visit us at www.tigertalesbooks.com

A Friend for Bear

by Steve Smallman   Illustrated by Caroline Pedler

tiger tales

DISCARDED
from Iowa City Public Library

IOWA CITY

NOV -- 2020

PUBLIC LIBRARY

All through the long, cold winter,
Bear had slept safe and snug in
her den.

Then, at last, a warm breeze
melted away the forest frost.
Bear's eyes blinked open, and she
bounced out of bed!

"IT'S SPRING!" she cried, racing outside.
Everything was fresh, and green, and sparkly.
Bear felt dizzy with the joy of it all!
"I WANT TO RUN, AND JUMP, AND SMELL
FLOWERS, AND TICKLE TADPOLES!"
she shouted.

"And I can't forget TWIRLING!"
She twirled around so fast . . .

she tripped over a stone!
But it wasn't a stone.

It was a tortoise.

"Oops-a-daisy!" said Tortoise.
"Are you all right?"

"I was just twirling!" said Bear.
"Because IT'S SPRIIIIIIIIIIIIIIIING! Next I'm
going to roll down a hill, climb trees, and
make new friends."

"That sounds wonderful," beamed Tortoise.

"Come with me!" suggested Bear.

"Oh, I couldn't keep up," sighed Tortoise.
"I only have little legs."

"That's okay," laughed Bear, lifting
Tortoise up. "I'll give you a piggyback ride."
And off they went.

"Look at us go!" laughed Tortoise. "I've never moved so fast!"

"Can we play?" called two fox cubs. But Bear galloped right past them.

"Bear!" cried Tortoise, "I thought making new friends was on your list."

"It is!" replied Bear. "But I haven't finished running yet!"

They burst into a meadow.

"Can't we stop and smell the flowers?" pleaded Tortoise.

"No time to stop—too much to do!" laughed Bear. "Start smelling!"

"Ouch!" grumbled Tortoise as a bumblebee bounced off his head. "My nose doesn't work at this speed!"

But Bear was running too fast to hear him.

Bear finally skidded to a halt
at the top of a small hill.
Tortoise looked around in wonder.
"I've never been so high!" he gasped.
"I can see the world! Thank you, Bear.
This is perfect."

"PERFECT FOR ROLLING!" finished
Bear. And clutching Tortoise tightly, she
rolled over and over, all the way
down the hill.

They stopped with a bump at
the foot of a tall tree.

"Time to climb!" declared Bear.

"Oh, no," groaned Tortoise, his head
spinning. "Can't I just sit—"

"—ON MY
SHOULDERS?
GOOD IDEA!"
finished Bear.
And up they went!

Mommy Bird was very surprised!
"Shoo!" she flapped.
"Time to go!" whispered Tortoise.
"TIME TO TICKLE TADPOLES!"
bellowed Bear. "TO THE POND!"

"What a day!" puffed Tortoise as he flopped down by the water's edge. Bear dropped down beside him. They watched ducklings and tadpoles playing in the water.

"Are you thinking what I'm thinking?" asked Bear.

"Yes," sighed Tortoise dreamily. "This is the perfect spot . . ."

". . . TO JUMP FROM!" cheered Bear.
Then, she grabbed Tortoise and leaped into the pond!

"Wasn't that great?" laughed Bear, scrambling out.

But Tortoise had had enough. "NO!" he spluttered.
"I CAN'T SWIM! MY SHELL IS FULL OF WATER, AND
I HAVE WEEDS UP MY NOSE!"

"But you wanted to swim!" said Bear in surprise.

"NO I DID NOT!" snorted Tortoise.

"You haven't stopped to listen, look, or make friends," he finished.

"But there's SO much to do!" cried Bear. "I can't stop!"

"Well, you'll have to," declared Tortoise, "because it's bedtime!"

"NOOOOOOOOOOO!" howled Bear. "I'M NOT TIRED! I DON'T WANT TO GO BACK TO BED FOREVER AND EVER! I WANT IT TO BE SPRING AGAIN!"

"Oh, Bear," smiled Tortoise,
"it's not time to hibernate yet!
Tomorrow will still be spring."
"It will?" sniffled Bear. "And then
I can run, and twirl, and climb?"

"Yes!" nodded Tortoise. "And maybe sit
and watch, too!"

"Do you think I might make some
friends?" Bear whispered.

"I'm sure you will!" chuckled Tortoise.
"You already found one today!"

"I have?" asked Bear. "Who?"

"Me, Bear," said Tortoise. "Me."

Bear beamed. "Can I give you a ride back home?"
"Will it be another fast ride?" asked Tortoise.
"No," chuckled Bear, "let's go slowly this time,
I want to smell the flowers!"

So as the sun set, the two friends wandered
slowly all the way home to bed.